The Thank You Book

Mary Lyn Ray

Illustrated by Stephanie Graegin

Houghton Mifflin Harcourt
Boston   New York

For all the thank yous there are to say. —*M.L.R.*

To Bustopher, the greatest cat in the whole wide world. —*S.G.*

Text copyright © 2018 by Mary Lyn Ray
Illustrations copyright © 2018 by Stephanie Graegin

hmhco.com

The illustrations in this book were done in pencil and watercolor and assembled and colored digitally.
The text type was set in Adobe Caslon Pro.
Hand lettering by Leah Palmer Preiss

Library of Congress Cataloging-in-Publication Data is on file.

ISBN: 978-0-544-79136-7

Manufactured in China
SCP 10 9 8 7 6 5 4 3 2 1
4500710940

Thank you isn't just for learning manners.
It's also for when something wakes a
little hum—a happy little hum—inside you
and you want to answer back.

So when the sun brings a new day,
a *thank you* is for morning.

Another is for cup and plate.

Thank you is for buzz and bloom
and grass (and toes)

and all that makes us wonder.

And it's, besides, for swings and slides.

Thank you is for glue and glitter

and for learning something new.

It's for parades.

And it's for puddles.

Thank you is for laps

and books.

WITHDRAWN

It's for having birthdays.
And for birthday cake.

It's also for when hurt or sad

or not-so-good gets better.

It's for zippers that zip jackets

when warm days turn to cold—

and for the year's surprises
before green days come back.

Thank you is for hats and mittens.
It's for hands to hold.

Thank you is for family.

Thank you is for home.

It's for this earth we ride on,
and for the stars beyond.

Thank you is for bathtub boats
and for bubble bath.

It's for pajamas
and more stories

and for
go to sleep now kisses.

Then in the dark it's for a light

and for knowing morning
will come after night.

It's for what we give a name to
and for what we can't.

Still, it's all we feel inside us
that makes us glad
that we are us.

So for what's big and for what's small
and all that's in between,
every day or special day,
we wrap a hug around each day—
to say another *thank you*.